Woolly Jumpers

Woolly Jumpers

Written and illustrated by
Peta Blackwell

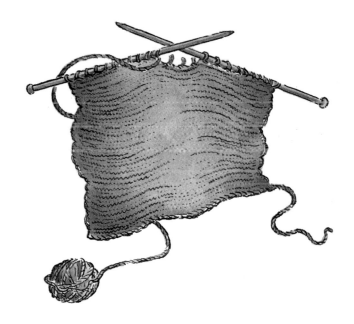

PUFFIN BOOKS

For Mark and Daisy Bridle
Thank you Carolyn Dinan
Thank you Elizabeth Hawkins

PUFFIN BOOKS

Published by the Penguin Group
Penguin Books Ltd, 80 Strand, London WC2R 0RL, England
Penguin Putnam Inc., 375 Hudson Street, New York, New York 10014, USA
Penguin Books Australia Ltd, 250 Camberwell Road, Camberwell, Victoria 3124, Australia
Penguin Books Canada Ltd, 10 Alcorn Avenue, Toronto, Ontario, Canada M4V 3B2
Penguin Books India (P) Ltd, 11 Community Centre, Panchsheel Park, New Delhi – 110 017, India
Penguin Books (NZ) Ltd, Cnr Rosedale and Airborne Roads, Albany, Auckland, New Zealand
Penguin Books (South Africa) (Pty) Ltd, 24 Sturdee Avenue, Rosebank 2196, South Africa

Penguin Books Ltd, Registered Offices: 80 Strand, London WC2R 0RL, England

www.penguin.com

First published 1998
9 10 8

Printed and bound in China by Leo Paper Products Ltd

0–140–38703–X

Mabel Cablestitch loved to knit. In her
house there were knitted carpets,
knitted cushions, knitted chairs, and
even a big knitted sofa. Mabel knitted
because she was lonely and it helped
pass the time.

"I do like knitting," said Mabel.
Clickety-click! Clickety-click! went
the needles. Clickety-click-clack-SNAP!
The needles had broken.

"Ravelling ribstitch!" Mabel exclaimed
crossly. "Now what shall I do?"

Just then there was a knock at the door.

Rat-a-tat-tat!

"Hang on, dearie!" called Mabel. "I'll be there in a minute."

She hobbled to the door and opened it cautiously.

There stood a young man with a large open suitcase.

"Could I interest you in a handy pocket-sized radio?" he asked. "Or maybe you'd like these lovely clip-on earrings?"

"Not really," Mabel replied. She peered at his junk. "But I could do with some new knitting needles."

"I have just the thing," said the young man. He handed Mabel a pair of old wooden needles. "Happy knitting," he said brightly. And he sauntered out of the gate with a whistle.

Mabel looked at the needles thoughtfully.

"They are very old," she said to herself. "I wonder if they are any good?"

She took a ball of wool from her basket and sat down in her favourite knitted chair.

Clickety-click! Clickety-click! went
the needles. Clickety-clack! Clickety
. . . Clock!

CLICK . . . CLOCK!

The sound had lulled her to sleep.

Mabel woke with a start. She leapt
out of her chair.

"Jumping jerseys! A WOOLLY
CAT!" she cried. "Where on earth
have you come from?"

The cat just sat there.

"Well, I've always wanted a bit of
company," Mabel told the cat. "I'll
knit you a blanket to sleep on. And I'd
better give you a proper name. I shall
call you Mitten."

That night, Mabel went to sleep in her knitted bed. Mitten went to sleep on his knitted blanket. But the needles continued to knit all by themselves.

The next morning the house shook
with a strange noise.

"RAARGH!"

"That can't be the alarm clock,"
yawned Mabel.
"RAAARGH!"

"You do sound hungry, Mitten," she
said to her cat.

"RAAAARGH!"

"Perhaps I left the television on? I'll go and see."

Mabel went down to the front room and opened the door. She came face to face with . . .

A HUGE WOOLLY TIGER!

"Bobbles above!" shrieked Mabel.
She slammed the door and scuttled
into the kitchen. She was so frightened,
she stayed there all day.

"Tiger or no tiger," she declared, "I
must find those needles. Or goodness
knows what they'll knit next!"

That night, Mabel went to sleep in her knitted bed. Mitten went to sleep on his knitted blanket. But the needles continued to knit all by themselves.

The following day strange noises
came from every room.

"OOO! OOO! OOO!"

"Is someone in my bedroom?"
whispered Mabel.

SPLISH! SPLOSH!

"Who's in the bathroom?" she
squeaked.

Clickety-click! Clickety-click!

"Is the tap dripping? I'll go and see."

She hobbled to the kitchen. She
opened the door. She came face to
face with . . .

A GIGANTIC WOOLLY
ELEPHANT!

"The needles!" cried Mabel.
She snatched them from the
elephant.

At that moment, she heard a knock at the door. Rat-a-tat-tat!

Mabel jerked the door open. It was the young man again.

"Greetings!" he said, as cheery as ever. "Would you like some more needles?"

"No, I wouldn't!" spluttered Mabel. "You can have this pair back."

She handed the needles to the young man.

"My house isn't big enough for all these animals. I'm sorry, but they'll all have to go!"

The young man looked
very surprised. For once he
was lost for words.

Rat-a-tat-tat!

The young man was still standing outside the front door. But all the animals had changed into little toys!

They were now all in the suitcase, looking very glum indeed. "Can I give you this as a little present?" the young man asked.

He handed Mabel a small woolly elephant.

"I've told you," said Mabel. "I don't have room for an elephant."

And she shut the door with a bang.

"I'll call again soon," said the voice through the letterbox. "Ta-ta for now!"

Mabel marched into her kitchen.

"I need a nice cup of tea to calm me down," she said to herself.

The house seemed very quiet now, and empty. Mabel felt sad.

"If only I hadn't given Mitten away," she sniffed. "I do miss that cat."

"Yards of yarn! It's Mitten!" cried
Mabel. "Oh Mitten, I am glad to see
you!" She picked up the cat and
hugged him. Mabel was never lonely
ever again.

DUMPLING
Dick King-Smith

Dumpling wishes she could be long and sausage-shaped like other dachshunds. When a witch's cat grants her wish, Dumpling becomes the longest dog ever.

BELLA AT THE BALLET
Brian Ball

Bella has been looking forward to her first ballet lesson for ages – but she's cross when Mum says Baby Tommy is coming with them. Bella is sure Tommy will spoil everything, but in the end it's hard to know who enjoys the class more – Bella or Tommy!

BEAR'S BAD MOOD
John Prater

Bear is cross. His father wakes him up much too early, his favourite breakfast cereal has run out and his sisters hold a pillow-fight in his room. Even when his friends arrive, Bear just doesn't feel like playing. Instead, he runs away – and a wonderful chase begins!